For the greatest grandmother,
my mother — RY

Text copyright © 2018 by Jairo Buitrago
Illustrations copyright © 2018 by Rafael Yockteng
Translation copyright © 2018 by Elisa Amado
Published in Canada and the USA in 2018 by Groundwood Books

Groundwood Books / House of Anansi Press
groundwoodbooks.com

We acknowledge the Government of Canada for its financial support
of our publishing program.

With the participation of the Government of Canada
Avec la participation du gouvernement du Canada | Canadä

Library and Archives Canada Cataloguing in Publication
Buitrago, Jairo
[Al otro lado del jardín. English]
On the other side of the garden / Jairo Buitrago ; [illustrated
by] Rafael Yockteng ; [translated by] Elisa Amado.
Translation of: Al otro lado del jardín.
Issued in print and electronic formats.
ISBN 978-1-55498-983-6 (hardcover). — ISBN 978-1-55498-984-3 (PDF)
I. Yockteng, Rafael, illustrator II. Amado, Elisa, translator
III. Title. IV. Title: Al otro lado del jardín. English.
PZ7.B8857On 2018   j863'.7   C2017-905235-7
C2017-905236-5

The illustrations were created digitally.
Design by Michael Solomon
Printed and bound in Malaysia

MIX
Paper from
responsible sources
FSC
www.fsc.org   FSC® C012700

JAIRO BUITRAGO

On the OTHER SIDE *of the* GARDEN

PICTURES BY
RAFAEL YOCKTENG

TRANSLATED BY
ELISA AMADO

GROUNDWOOD BOOKS
HOUSE OF ANANSI PRESS
TORONTO   BERKELEY

I was looking out the window, so I didn't pay attention to what my dad was saying.

Dad's car pulled away. I stood there and
watched it go. Then we climbed up the steps.

My bedroom wasn't my bedroom. No sounds could be heard outside, only my grandmother's steps in the hall.

I lay down on the bed that wasn't my bed, thinking about the city, about my friends who were far away now, and that Dad would have to come back and get me some day.

And when three creatures stare at you
through a window, all you can do is open it
and talk to them.

"Good evening," said the owl.

"Are you new here?" asked the frog.

"Who are you? Have you got any bread or cookies?" said the mouse.

"I am Isabel," I answered, "and I don't have any bread or cookies."

The moon was huge and bright, so I could see them clearly. They looked like pretty good guys. I thought it would be okay to go for a walk with them. It was a beautiful night, and I wasn't sleepy.

We slid off the roof quietly so we wouldn't wake up Grandmother.

The fresh grass felt cold to my feet.
I told them that in the city I hardly
ever go barefoot. It's different. There's
not much green to stand on.

"I don't know the city," stated the owl.

"Why haven't we seen you before?" asked the frog.

"Maybe, later, you could give me some milk?" said the mouse.

"I lived in another place before," I answered, "but Dad has left me here for a few days. He'll come and get me soon."

We walked past all kinds of bushes and flowers.
The owl knew all their names. She was clever. The
frog pointed out the stars in the sky.

"We'll walk to the creek, a little farther along," said the owl.

"The creek is my house," explained the frog. "How about you? How come you don't live with your parents?"

"Later, maybe, we could eat something at your house," said the mouse timidly.

"I used to live with Mum and Dad," I answered, "and this house isn't my house. It's Grandmother's house."

Then we sat on the edge of the creek and put our feet in the water.

"I've known your grandmother for many years," said the owl.

"No one ever comes to visit her. You are the first, I think," said the frog.

"She's kind. Sometimes she leaves out crumbs and rice in the garden for us," said the mouse.

"You sure talk a lot!" I said to them.

Then we climbed a small hill. From there we could see the house. Grandmother's house.

"I'm glad the grandmother has company," said the owl, with what might have been a smile.

"For sure you have to stay with her for a while," said the frog.

"Sometimes we have a picnic on this hill," said the mouse. "You're invited."

Suddenly I was telling them about me.

"Mum went to live and work in
another country. Dad and I stayed
behind, just the two of us. I hardly even
remembered that I had a grandmother.
I'd only ever seen her in some pictures."

We walked along a wooden fence. I told them more about my mum and the letters she sends me, and that my dad is looking for work.

The three of them listened as we walked and walked.

A soft, chilly little breeze began to blow. We snuggled up to stay warm and looked out over the still countryside that lay beyond.

"Never cross this fence, Isabel," warned the owl. "There are some fierce dogs on the other side."

"And they bite," said the frog.

"Sometimes I sneak across to eat a little of their food. So if you want to go over there, I can keep watch so they don't appear all of a sudden," offered the mouse.

The sky was getting light and faraway birds were beginning to sing. The owl, the frog and the mouse went and hid in the bushes.

"Goodbye, Isabel," said the owl.

"If you'd like we can see you again by the creek," said the frog.

"You'd better get home for breakfast," said the mouse.

"Goodbye," I said, a little frightened. And I ran toward the house on my muddy legs.

Grandmother was waiting for me by the door.

She asked me if I was a sleepwalker. And she didn't scold me. She hugged me tight to her chest. She is tall and strong, like me.

"You know you are going to be here for quite a while?" she asked.

"Yes, Grandmother," I said. I felt like crying. "Can I walk in your garden at night?"

"At night and in the day. This is your house, too."

She gave me milk and bread and jam and then
showed me her flowers. The garden looked different in
the daylight. The sun warmed my back and my cold feet.

Arm in arm, we walked back to the wooden
fence. She showed me some thorny bushes, which
grow wild.

"There, on the other side of the garden, if you
look carefully and don't make noise, you might see
some animals."

"I'd like to see them every day, Grandmother," I said.

GARDEN INVENTORY

THE PLANTS

This is the garden.

Its yellow flowers smell good. They fall, and the wind carries them away.

Behind the house, a plum tree, an elder bush and a cherry tree shade the smaller plants: sage, mint, thyme and rosemary that Grandmother uses in her cooking. And there is an old lemon tree that still produces lemons.

Twined on the fences are thorny wild blackberries and some bougainvillea and passion-fruit vines.

There is a solitary kumquat whose fruit, partly eaten by small bats, is always lying on the ground below. And in the distance, beyond the fence, there is a huge oak that stands up against the wind that comes down from the mountain at night.

There are other trees and shrubs, planted or wild: everlasting flowers, cacti, Judas trees, a poplar, wartweed. Grandmother tells me their names.

I didn't used to think much about trees or plants. Now they appear in my dreams all the time — they wrap themselves around my legs; they keep me company.

THE ANIMALS

A family of field mice comes and goes. They hide in the vines, where they are invisible. They collect grains and seeds. The cat sits in the window and from behind the glass watches them appear and disappear for hours and hours.

Sometimes, very early, it's possible to see a possum or a rabbit along the road.

And there are hundreds of birds: bluebirds, flycatchers, swallows, jays, blackbirds.

The old tree stumps are teeming with ants that bite bare feet. And butterflies and bumblebees search the birdfeeders for their share.

Shy creatures flee the light when you gently lift a stone.

And a small falcon floats in the currents of air that move through the clear sky — the Holy Spirit, my grandmother calls it.

When night falls, there are many other animals that we can't see. Frogs and cicadas sing. We close the windows.